THIS BLOOMSBURY BOOK

BELONGS TO

....

traffic circle

shop vet post office

school

Chester's house

dinosaur park

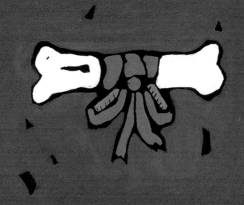

To my grandparents – O V

First published in Great Britain in 2001 by Bloomsbury Publishing Plc
38 Soho Square, London, W1D 3HB
This paperback edition first published in 2002

Copyright © Olivia Villet 2001
The moral right of the author/illustrator has been asserted

A CIP catalogue record of this book is available from the British Library
ISBN 0 7475 5564 8

Printed in Belgium by Proost
1 3 5 7 9 10 8 6 4 2

Chester's
Big Surprise

OLIVIA VILLET

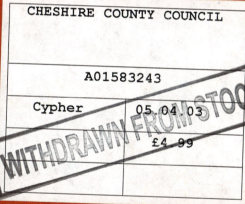

BLOOMSBURY
CHILDREN'S
BOOKS

Chester and Tilda are best friends.
Every day they go to the traffic
circle to play.

Today Tilda hasn't come out. Chester isn't happy, he's feeling rather lonely.

'There's a cloud that looks like Tilda,' sighs Chester. 'Could Tilda have changed her mind? I'm going to look for her.'

Maybe Tilda's
at the shop?

Chester looks
inside.

He looks under the table
and between the shelves.

He doesn't find Tilda, but he does find an old peanut butter sandwich.

Chester runs outside.
There's Sharky.

Maybe he knows
where Tilda is.

Sharky doesn't know where Tilda is, but he does want Chester's sandwich. Chester gulps it down before Sharky can eat it.

Hey, I have an idea where Tilda might be, thinks Chester as he reaches the school.

Inside the gates, the children pat and rub Chester. This is great!

He remembers that he must look for Tilda. She's not here.

Chester looks into the dinosaur park.
It is dark and scary in the
dinosaur park.

Is Tilda inside?
Did that one move?

Before Chester can run away
he sees Pete.

'Hello, Chester,' says Pete.
'Are you ready to go home now?'

When Chester and Pete get home, Chester hears a funny noise.

'Gggrr,' says Chester. 'Gggrr, gggrr. What's making that noise?'

It's Tilda and she's got a surprise for Chester.

What a wonderful surprise!

traffic circle

shop 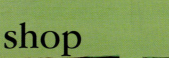 vet post office

Chester's house

school

dinosaur park

Enjoy more great picture books from Bloomsbury ...

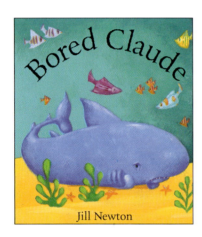

Bored Claude

Jill Newton

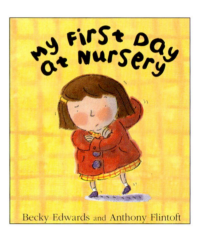

My First Day at Nursery

Becky Edwards & Anthony Flintoft

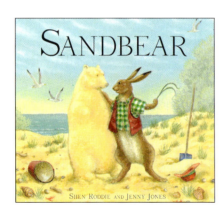

Sandbear

Shen Roddie & Jenny Jones

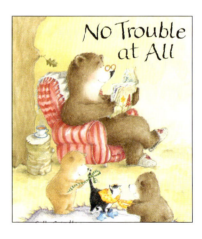

No Trouble at All

Sally Grindley & Eleanor Taylor